I was halfway home when a speeding streak cut right in front of my bike.

I hit the brakes so hard that I flew right over the handlebars. Suddenly hands picked me up by the shirt and waved me around like a wet towel. "Come on, Elliot," Justin Ambrose said. His face was so close to mine that I could smell the fresh wad of strawberry bubble gum he was chewing. "I wanted us to be friends. What kind of a friend are you if you catch my fly balls and put me out in baseball games?"

I thought he wanted me to answer him. But before I could, a sharp pain exploded in my stomach. I gasped and doubled over. Justin lifted me up again.

"You don't understand, do you?"

I didn't understand anything. I couldn't. My stomach hurt too much and I couldn't breathe.

"Friends help each other out," Justin said. He dropped me to the ground. "Right?"

"I don't want to be your friend," I gasped.

Justin laughed. "Elliot, you don't want to be my enemy."

How I Survived Fifth Grade

*Megan Stine and
H. William Stine*

Cover by Susan Tang

Troll Associates

Library of Congress Cataloging-in-Publication Data

Stine, Megan.
    How I survived fifth grade / by Megan Stine and H. William Stine.
       p.   cm.—(Making the grade)
    Summary: Elliot doubts that he will survive the fifth grade,
because the obnoxious class bully has selected him as his own
special victim.
    ISBN 0-8167-2386-9 (lib. bdg.)   ISBN 0-8167-2387-7 (pbk.)
    [1. Bullies—Fiction. 2. Schools—Fiction.] I. Stine, H.
William. II. Title. III. Series: Making the grade (Mahwah, N.J.)
PZ7.S86035Ho 1992
[Fic]—dc20   90-26790

A TROLL BOOK, published by Troll Associates

Printed in the United States of America.

10 9 8 7 6 5 4 3

How I Survived
Fifth Grade

For Charlene and Herb Solomon,
who truly understand the need for laughter.

Chapter 1

Maybe there really were some advantages to being the smallest kid in the fifth grade. But I couldn't think of any. I couldn't get over the fact that there were fourth graders who were bigger than I was. And to be honest, I could think of a couple of third graders who came pretty close, too.

I'm ten years old now, and all my life I've been at least two growth spurts behind all of my friends. In kindergarten and first grade, kids would call me names like "shorty" or "shrimp toast" or "Little PeeWee"—as if PeeWee wasn't bad enough.

But somewhere around second grade, I learned to laugh about it. For example, I laughed when Marissa Grimble said to me, "Gee, Elliot, I have a *doll* that wears clothes the same size as yours."

And, in the fourth grade, I laughed when my best friend, Carlo, came up with what he called a scientific explanation for my small size.

"Elliot," he said, "I've solved the mystery about why you're so short. You're the smartest kid in the class, right? So I figure your brain is growing so incredibly fast it's eating up all the neutrinos and neutrino-ettes before your body can get any."

Believe it or not, that really *was* Carlo's idea of a scientific explanation.

However, this year in the fifth grade at Southside Elementary School, something happened that I couldn't laugh about. Justin Ambrose.

Who or what was Justin Ambrose? A crazed, bloodthirsty killer from a horror movie? A rare and fatal childhood disease?

Both those guesses are close, except Justin Ambrose was worse. Big time worse.

Worse because he was the school bully. He singlehandedly redefined the word *mean*.

Every year since second grade Justin had picked someone—"a total pinhead," in Justin's words. And then he stayed on the kid's case the whole school year. I had never been in Justin's class before, so he had never had the opportunity to pick on me. But when I saw him standing in my classroom on the first day of fifth grade, my heart sank. From the look on his face, it was painfully clear to me that I was going to be this year's pinhead.

I found out for sure after school when Justin grabbed my backpack away from me as Carlo and I were going home. It was a tricky move because Carlo and I were riding our bikes. But Justin was big and he was fast.

He zoomed up beside me on his skateboard and, in one powerful tug, he had my backpack off. He then tossed it over a fence and into the front yard where Mutt and Jeff lived. Mutt and Jeff are two identical, and seriously mean, dogs.

Mutt immediately clamped his teeth on one shoulder strap of my pack and Jeff chomped down on the other. And then they started shaking their heads and having an angry, noisy tug-of-war.

I don't know which dog won, but my backpack definitely lost. In seconds it was scattered across the yard in small yellow, green, and black nylon shreds.

Before I could say anything, Justin shoved me. "It's only the beginning, Elliot."

I looked up into his face. The sun sparkled off his blond crewcut. He was beaming with pride.

"Why me, Justin?" I asked.

"We're going to be pals, Elliot. I'm going to stick to you like Velcro," he said with a laugh. Then he took off on his skateboard. "Best buddies for sure," he called back to me.

"I have my doubts," I sighed to Carlo.

But Justin was right about one thing. It was only the beginning. On the second day of school, he somehow convinced our teacher, Ms. Wilson, that he couldn't see the chalkboard from where he sat and that he should sit in the desk directly behind me. She let him change his seat. Then he spent the rest of the morning sliding his desk back and forth, ramming me hard in the back.

At lunch that day I sat down across the table from Carlo, hoping he would help me figure out what to do about Justin. "Carlo . . ." I started to say.

But before I could say anything else, I noticed that Carlo couldn't stop coughing. "What's wrong with you?" I asked.

Carlo didn't answer. He kept coughing and choking. His face even started to turn a little blue. I jumped out of my chair and rushed around behind Carlo, wrapping my arms around him. I wasn't sure I could do the Heimlich Maneuver—you know, where you push on someone's abdomen when he's choking to make him spit out what's stuck in his throat. All I knew was I had to do *something* to save my best friend's life.

I started to squeeze hard. "Let go!" Carlo said, not coughing at all. "You made me blow it! I was just about to set the world record for choking in a school cafeteria."

More than anything in life, Carlo wanted to set a record that would get him into the *Guinness Book of World Records*. He dreamed about it, and plotted about it night and day.

The only problem was that some of his ideas for world records were really crazy. For instance, one time he tried to set a world record for taking the most out-of-focus photos of his family on a single trip to the Grand Canyon. Another time he claimed he set a record for playing the longest "air-guitar" solo.

"Forget the *Guinness Book* for a minute," I said. "What am I going to do about Justin Ambrose?"

Carlo thought about my question while he ate a bite of his sandwich without choking once. "Justin Ambrose is a bully with the brain power of a dog biscuit," he said finally. "There's only one thing you can do, Elliot."

"What's that?"

"Keep out of his way."

Easier said than done, I thought. But it sounded like good advice. I decided to give it a try.

After lunch our class went to gym. The teacher, Mr. Douchet, had us choose sides for a baseball game. As soon as Justin was chosen for one team, I volunteered for the other team. Carlo and I gave each other high fives as I walked over to stand with him.

"Way to go, Elliot!" Carlo said in a quiet voice. "That's what I meant about keeping out of Justin's way."

I'm pretty good at baseball. But that doesn't mean I don't take my usual share of abuse for being short. That day Hank McCord was pitching. Hank's the kind of kid who can never resist making a joke about me being small.

When I came up to bat in the third inning, Hank shouted, "Batter up!"

Of course, I was already standing at the plate waiting for the first pitch.

"Batter up!" Hank shouted again.

"Give me a break, Hank, and throw the ball," I shouted back.

Hank squinted down in my direction from the pitcher's mound. "Hey, is that you, Elliot?" he said. "Sorry, bud, I couldn't see you."

While everyone was laughing, I took a couple of practice swings. When the first pitch came, I smacked the ball as hard as I could into left field. A bigger kid could probably have legged it into a double, but

I had to settle for a single—and two RBI's. I put our team ahead 6 to 5.

And that was still the score when the other team came up to bat in the last inning. I was playing right field that day. It was always so quiet out in right field that I considered bringing a book to read just to have something to do.

The other team put two kids on base but then we struck out two batters. If we could get the next batter out, we'd win the game.

So guess who the next batter was? Justin Ambrose, of course.

The three of us in the outfield started backing up. We knew that Justin could hit the ball hard.

Sure enough, Justin hit the first pitch. The ball sailed through the air. Suddenly I realized that it was going to fall about fifteen feet in front of me.

I took off, running as fast as I could, and leaped into the air with my arms outstretched. I hit the ground on my stomach, but when I looked in my glove I was holding the ball. I had caught it! Justin was out and our team had won the game!

My team was cheering and pounding me on the back.

"Game's over! Everybody inside!" shouted Mr. Douchet, blowing his whistle. "Time to go back to class!"

As everyone in my class headed back toward the school building, Justin hung back a little and walked slowly toward me.

"Elliot," he said. His cold blue eyes looked straight at me. "That should have been a home run. My team lost because of you." He glared at me even harder. "Big mistake."

"It's only a game, Justin," I said. "It doesn't count."

"Everything *you* do counts." Justin pointed at me. "See you after school, cream cheese." Then he ran back into the building.

At first I tried to laugh it off. "What's he going to do?" I asked Carlo. "Push me down? Hit me a couple of times?"

"Yeah, sure," Carlo said.

I could tell that Carlo was trying to sound encouraging. But then he added, "I wonder what the world record is for being punched?"

Whatever the record was, I knew I didn't want to tie it, break it, or even challenge it—not with Justin Ambrose.

I'm not a coward and everyone knows that. I have been in some fights. However, when you're on the small side of the growth charts there just aren't many fights you can win.

So when the bell rang at the end of school, I hurried out of the classroom. I figured if I got a head start maybe I could avoid whatever pain and torture Justin had planned for me.

I raced to my locker and threw my books in the plastic bag I had been using ever since yesterday when my backpack was torn to shreds. Then I quickly unlocked my bike from the bike rack.

But I wasn't fast enough.

I was halfway home when a speeding streak cut right in front of my bike. I hit the brakes so hard that I flew right over the handlebars. I crashed to the ground, dazed. From behind me I heard the scrape of a skateboard coming to a quick stop.

Suddenly hands picked me up by the shirt and waved me around like a wet towel.

"Come on, Elliot," Justin Ambrose said. His face was so close to mine that I could smell the fresh wad of strawberry bubble gum he was chewing. "I wanted us to be friends. What kind of a friend are you if you catch my fly balls and put me out in baseball games?"

I thought he wanted me to answer him. But before I could, a sharp pain exploded in my stomach. I gasped and doubled over. Justin lifted me up again.

"You understand, don't you?"

I didn't understand anything. I couldn't. My stomach hurt too much and I couldn't breathe.

"Friends help each other out," Justin said. He dropped me to the ground. "Right?"

"I don't want to be your friend," I gasped.

Justin laughed. "Elliot, you don't want to be my enemy."

He kicked my bicycle into the street and took off for home.

Chapter 2

Justin Ambrose had hit me so hard he'd knocked the wind out of me. No one had ever done that before. But what made everything worse was knowing that he might do it again. And that there was no way I could stop him.

I picked myself up off the ground. My stomach hurt a lot. I wanted to cry. My whole body seemed to be telling me to cry, but I wouldn't. I slowly walked over to my bike and pulled it out of the street. Walking it home, I thought about what had happened and what it meant.

I was a foot shorter and forty pounds

lighter than Justin. In short—excuse the pun—I might as well walk around wearing a sign that said, "Perfect target. Bullies please form a single line."

That night dinner was pretty quiet. I sat staring at my plate and pushing the food into separate piles with my fork. I didn't feel like eating and I really didn't feel like talking. I should add that *both* are serious crimes in my house.

"Elliot," my mom said, trying to snap me to attention, "you look like you're waiting for your food to invite you to eat it."

My dad laughed. He loves to laugh. He'll laugh at almost anything, even my mom's lamest jokes.

So I laughed, too, trying to fool them into thinking nothing was wrong. I also hoped to keep them from asking me any more questions.

But who was I kidding? My parents spend their whole lives asking questions. My mom's a divorce lawyer and my dad's a child psychologist. Telling my parents not to ask questions would be like telling a bee to stay away from flowers.

"Well, how was school?" my father asked.

"School was . . . okay," I said, trying to think of something positive.

The last thing I wanted to talk about was my new after-school activity—being Justin Ambrose's punching bag. It's not that my parents wouldn't be sympathetic. They would be. In fact, that was the whole problem. They'd be so sympathetic, and worry so much, they'd put me under twice as much pressure to do something about Justin. And I was under enough pressure already. Besides, admitting to my mom and dad that another kid had beaten me up was really humiliating.

"Well, here's something interesting," I said, trying to smile. "I think the kids in my class are getting used to the fact that I go to a special math group for algebra. When they saw my homework assignment today, only five of them fainted."

I expected at least to get a laugh from my dad, but all I got was an "Uh-huh" from both of them. In my house, "Uh-huh" was the professional lawyer and child psychologist talk for "We know you're keeping something from us."

My mom's eyebrows wrinkled together. "Is anything wrong, dear?" she asked.

"Nothing's wrong, Mom." I couldn't possibly tell her the truth. "Nothing I can't handle."

"We don't doubt that for a second, Elliot," said my dad, giving me a confident smile. "But if something's going on, I think it would help if you talked about it."

I pushed myself away from the table. "Hey, nothing's going on. Really," I said. "I'm just not hungry and I've got a lot of homework."

"Elliot . . ." My dad started to tell me to sit down. I know that's what he was going to say, but then he suddenly changed his mind and his tone of voice. "You know," he said, "if you want to talk, we're always here."

Actually, that isn't quite true, I wanted to say. You're not always here.

Part of me wanted to tell them what had happened, just so they wouldn't be so worried. But another part of me wasn't ready. "Don't worry," I finally said. "I have your beeper numbers memorized."

For the next few days I held my breath, waiting to find out exactly what it meant to be Justin Ambrose's buddy of the year. I didn't have to wait long.

I found out it meant that sometimes you'd come to your locker and he'd be standing in front of it. And he wouldn't move and you couldn't make him. You'd tell him that you had to get your books, but he'd say you didn't. You'd tell him that you had to get your jacket and he'd say you didn't. You'd tell him that you could stand there longer than he could and he'd say *you* were looking for a fight.

Being Justin's buddy of the year meant that he'd sit one table away from you in the cafeteria and trip you when you walked past. It meant he'd grab things out of your hands whenever he wanted to and walk right in front of you when you were talking to someone else. In other words, he'd take every opportunity to remind you that you were smaller, slower, and weaker than he was.

It didn't take the rest of the kids in my class long to realize what was going on. They soon figured out that I was Justin's "special buddy." I could tell they felt bad for me. But not bad enough to tell Justin to leave me alone. No one wanted to do that for one very good reason. It would have been an invitation to trade places with me.

I did have two friends who stood by me, especially when Justin was being his most obnoxious, which was only during the hours he was awake. Carlo was one of my defenders. The other one was my teacher, Ms. Wilson. But to tell you the truth, I wished they'd both just give up. Their help wasn't doing any good.

One time in gym when Justin had me pinned to the ground—which wasn't really part of the game, since we were playing volleyball at the time—Carlo shouted, "Justin, you bozo! You think you're frightening Elliot, don't you? But you're not!"

I don't know what made Carlo think I wasn't frightened. I knew for a fact that I was scared to death.

But what Ms. Wilson did was even worse. She really liked me, and I found out why one morning when she and I had a private conversation on the playground. She told me that when she was a kid, she was smart, too, and everyone in class hated her for it. So she knew exactly how I felt.

I shook my head in surprise. "Everyone in class likes me," I explained.

"Well, what about Justin?" Ms. Wilson asked.

"Yeah, you're right," I admitted with an embarrassed laugh. "I guess Justin does pretty much hate my guts."

"I thought he'd been giving you trouble," she said. "But from now on, don't worry about Justin. I'll handle him."

It turned out that her way of handling Justin was to tell him at least five times a day to leave me alone. This just made him hate me more. Then one day she totally exploded.

"Justin, stop it!" Ms. Wilson shouted.

Justin was behind me with a pair of scissors, offering to give me a crewcut on half of my head.

"Justin," Ms. Wilson yelled, "I'm not going to tell you again. Leave Elliot alone!"

"Oh, sure. Your little pet. That's great," he said with a nasty laugh.

Ms. Wilson's face turned red. At first I

thought she was embarrassed. Then I realized she was angry. "Justin, your behavior will not be tolerated!"

Justin didn't say a word and I was too nervous to turn around and look at him.

But a minute later, after everyone had settled down and gone back to work, he leaned forward and whispered in my ear, "Because of you, I was embarrassed in front of the whole class. Big mistake, Elliot."

Maybe Ms. Wilson thought she was pouring water on the fire, but I knew she was pouring gasoline. Now, Justin was going to fry me for sure.

Chapter 3

*T*he one bright spot came in October at the end of the month— Halloween. I was really looking forward to the idea of dressing up and pretending to be someone else. For my costume I decided to wear a striped prison uniform and tell everyone that I was an escaped convict— since that's how I felt a lot of the time these days.

Carlo, on the other hand, showed up at my house in no costume at all. Just jeans and a T-shirt. It was a first.

"This is going to be the greatest Halloween ever," Carlo announced.

He was moving fast and talking even faster. I knew this meant he had come up with another idea to achieve his dream of a lifetime—a place in the *Guinness Book of World Records*.

"You'll never guess what I thought up for tonight," he said.

Of course he had no intention of giving me a chance to guess.

"We're going after something tonight that no one's ever gone after before. *Candy*."

"Oh, right," I said. "As opposed to all those kids who trick-or-treat for socks and underwear."

He didn't laugh. "Elliot, where's your imagination?" Carlo said. "I'm talking about massive quantities of candy. More candy than anyone has ever collected in one Halloween night!"

He showed me his trick-or-treat bag. It was a stiff, department store shopping bag that had a second shopping bag inside. "Double-reinforced for extra strength," Carlo said.

The world record for the most trick-or-treat candy in one Halloween—it definitely sounded like a good idea to me.

I smiled at Carlo and got a second shopping bag out of the kitchen closet. Two seconds later, we were out the door.

I was in a great mood when we started out that Halloween. Some people think Carlo is a little strange because he's so obsessed about this world record thing. But that's one of the things I like most about Carlo. He has a goal and he's not going to stop until he gets it.

Besides, when he's in the middle of one of his schemes, he's funny to be with—so funny that it takes my mind off my problems.

That dark Halloween night I forgot all about Justin Ambrose. I stopped expecting him to jump out at me from behind every bush or tree. I stopped waiting for him to sweep by on his skateboard, punch me in the stomach, and ride off. Carlo and I had fun, just the way we used to.

Carlo was in great form that night, too.

"Oh, no! Don't tell me you're passing out Caribbean Bongo candy bars," Carlo said when we got to Mrs. McMeekin's house. She was a small, gray-haired woman who lived alone. He took the candy bar out of his shopping bag, which was more than half full by then, and pretended to check something on the label. "Didn't you hear?" he asked her. "These candy bars have been recalled."

"Really?" she said with concern.

"Yeah," Carlo answered. "They found rats living in the factory, nibbling the candy at night. Some of the rats fell into the vats and got stirred in with the chocolate."

"That's disgusting," shrieked Mrs. McMeekin.

"I know," Carlo said. "You should give me all of your Caribbean Bongo bars. I'll destroy them for you."

Carlo smiled as the woman dumped her entire bowl of candy into Carlo's bag.

The trick didn't work at too many houses, but it didn't matter. Carlo had lots of other stories.

His most successful one was "We're trick-

or-treating for all the kids in hospitals." He used that on several people. "We'll take them the candy tomorrow."

"That's really admirable," people said. "Take all the candy you want."

And, of course, he did.

As we walked away I mumbled. "Giving candy to hospital kids? You've never given anything away in your life."

"But I am, Elliot. I really am. See, first I set the world record for collecting the most candy. Then I set the world record for giving the most candy away—two records in one!"

We started back to my house. Our bags were really heavy. My two bags felt like they each weighed about twenty pounds.

Wouldn't it be fantastic, I thought, if Carlo really succeeded? If he really got his name in the *Guinness Book*?

I was daydreaming about Carlo's fame and glory as we walked through a dark neighborhood with plenty of huge trees. I guess that's why I didn't hear anything at first.

All of a sudden, out of nowhere, something jumped down from a tree limb that was hanging over the sidewalk. It was a werewolf! A huge, snarling werewolf! It shoved Carlo out of the way and then hit me in the stomach. "Big mistake, Elliot," growled the werewolf as I fell on the ground. I didn't have to guess twice—I knew what my mistake was. Being alive!

He started coming toward me while I was still on my back. The candy bags were beside me, with half the contents spilled all over the ground. I tried to scoot away as Justin leaned down to hit me again. But I couldn't move fast enough.

So I kicked at him—just to keep him away from me. My foot flew out and it landed right in his face. I had kicked Justin Ambrose in the mouth!

He tore off the thin rubber werewolf mask and I saw a wet, red line bubbling out of his lip. He was bleeding!

Oh, no, I thought. I'm dead meat now for sure.

I jumped to my feet and grabbed Carlo's arm. "Let's get out of here!" I said, pulling him with me down the street. For half a second, Carlo resisted. He didn't want to leave all that candy there. But then he heard Justin growl.

We ran as fast as we could without looking back, but we could hear Justin shouting behind us. "I'll pay you back, Elliot. Count on it, buddy!"

Chapter 4

"*D*ear Justin,"

For several days after Halloween I worked on writing a note. I wanted to explain to Justin on paper what I couldn't explain to him in person.

It's not that I didn't want to talk to him and settle our differences. But I knew what would happen if I approached him. And I already had one too many bruises.

Still, I wanted to explain certain things to him.

"Kicking you in the mouth was an accident," I wrote.

This was entirely true. Well, almost. I did

sort of enjoy seeing him bleed, especially after the weeks of threats and torture he put me through.

"I never intended to leave my footprint on your face. I believe physical violence always creates more problems than it solves."

It certainly was going to create more problems in my case. I knew that Justin would want revenge for being kicked. There was no way he'd settle for anything less than my blood.

"It's time for us to end this unpleasant situation and put our energy to better use."

In other words, I was getting tired of running from him.

After I wrote the note, I folded it and put it in an envelope. I went to school early and slipped the note through the air vent in Justin's locker door.

"What are you doing?" asked a voice from behind me.

My heart stopped. I turned around quickly. It was only Carlo.

"Carlo, don't scare me like that. I was just leaving a note in Justin's locker."

"Yeah?" Carlo said as we walked quickly down the hall toward our classroom. "What'd you say? Did you tell him you're going to part his hair with a chain saw?"

"Not exactly," I said.

"Did you tell him you're going to tighten his braces with a lug wrench?"

"Not exactly," I repeated, this time in a softer voice.

"Elliot, you didn't apologize for anything, did you?" He was looking at me as if I had just confessed to the crime of the century.

"Bad strategy?" I wondered out loud.

"Total one hundred percent wimpdom. It's like admitting that you're afraid of him and you're too weak to do anything about it."

"Well, it's the truth, Carlo. I can't hope for miracles. I can't grow a foot taller overnight. I can't develop a knockout punch with these hands. I'm still wearing a size small junior baseball glove."

Carlo suddenly grabbed my hands. He looked first at the backs, then turned them over and looked carefully at the palms. "A knockout punch?" he said. "Of course, you can develop a knockout punch."

"Sure, if I slip chemicals into Justin's fruit drink and turn him into a midget," I said.

"Hiiiyyaa!" Carlo shouted. His voice echoed through the school halls. He leaped into the air and came down ready to strike, legs spread and hands raised at me. "Karate! Elliot, you can take lessons like I do! All you have to do is enroll in the class for a while and you'll be able to take care of Justin superfast."

"Karate?" I asked. "Carlo, that's just breaking boards."

But after school that day I went with Carlo to Nick Subotnik's School of Flying Fists. The owner, Nick Subotnik, was a short, not-so-muscular man with a totally bald head and a very friendly smile. I asked him what karate was all about.

"It's not just breaking boards. It's the art of mental readiness," Nick said as he showed me his studio. It was a large room with ceiling-to-floor mirrors on all four walls. The hard wood floor was covered with large, thick, soft, red pads.

One by one, Nick's students came out of the dressing room wearing their Gis—the loose-fitting white martial arts jacket and pants. There were fifteen boys and girls of all ages and sizes. They all bowed to Nick before beginning their warm-up exercises.

"Karate is self-confidence," Nick told me. "It's an acceptance of the strengths you already have inside you."

I watched for a while as Carlo and the other kids followed Nick's instructions, stepping, kicking, yelling, slicing the air with their hands in incredibly fast motions.

Could I do that? Of course I could. I had to. Because if I worked hard and became strong and fast and confident, I'd never have to be afraid of Justin Ambrose again. In fact, he would have to watch out for *me*!

Two days later, after school, I reported to Nick Subotnik's School of Flying Fists, ready for action. I had a check signed by my dad for my first month's lessons. I had read and memorized eight books on martial arts, rented and watched three Chuck Norris movies, and bought my own Gi. Unfortunately, the pants were a little big on me. I wondered if I'd have to wear my beginner's white belt *and* suspenders.

Nick led the class through our exercises. I watched the other kids next to me and I watched Nick, too. He was small, but he moved gracefully. The one-on-one exercises were as exciting to watch as they were to be in. Two students bowed and then circled each other, sizing each other up and then exploding in a flurry of jabs and midair kicks and twirls.

After only a couple of lessons, Nick told me, "Elliot, I've never seen anyone learn so fast. You must really have your mind in the right place."

I didn't know if I had my mind in the right place. All I knew was that I had Justin Ambrose sitting behind me.

As for the letter I wrote him, Justin made copies of it and taped it everywhere around the school, including the girls' bathrooms. Let's put it this way: No one thought it was the best thing I'd ever written.

This may sound a little strange, but after my karate lessons I felt bigger. I felt as if my muscles and bones were stretching. This feeling was totally contradicted when I stepped on my dad's scale, which I did as soon as I got home after each lesson. My dad has one of those doctor's office scales that measure both weight and height.

According to the scale I was still the same shrimpy me on the outside. But not on the inside.

"Nick was right," I told Carlo one Saturday morning after a karate lesson. We were standing in my kitchen, starving, after our workout. "I'm getting in touch with the power inside me."

"That's great," Carlo said. "Now, how about getting in touch with the food inside the refrigerator?"

I opened the fridge, which was packed tight with food. My dad must have gone shopping while I was at the School of Flying Fists. "We have ham, turkey, Swiss cheese, goat cheese, tomatoes, three kinds of bread, five kinds of mustard, and three kinds of lettuce. You want it all?"

There was no answer. It definitely was not Carlo's style to be unable to make up his mind on what to eat.

"Did you faint from starvation?" I joked. Still there was no answer.

When I turned around, Carlo was doing something with his hands in midair. At first I thought it was karate. But then I looked more closely and realized that it wasn't karate at all. He was building an invisible sandwich in the air. Maybe he was hungrier than I thought.

The invisible sandwich grew taller and taller. When it got up to about his belt, Carlo turned to me with wild eyes and said, "It'll work, Elliot. Of course, it'll have to be bigger than this. Thirty feet at least."

"Carlo—what are you talking about?"

"My sandwich," he said. "I'm going to build the world's tallest club sandwich and set a record that will get me into the book!"

He didn't even have to say *Guinness Book* anymore. I knew what he was talking about.

"Carlo, aren't there already records for big sandwiches?"

"Long, not tall," Carlo said. "Come on, Elliot. Help me figure out how much stuff I'll need."

I did some quick math in my head and estimated about twenty-five loaves of bread, seventy-five pounds of sliced turkey and cheese, a bushel of tomatoes, three dozen heads of lettuce, and maybe fifty pounds of bacon.

But that wasn't the part that was hard to swallow about this sandwich. "Carlo," I said, sitting down at the table and grabbing a calculator, "do you know what it will cost to make this sandwich?"

Carlo put his hand over the calculator display. "Don't worry about details, Elliot. I'll get the money. Just keep thinking about one thing—making history."

Well, that was okay for Carlo. He could go through life thinking about nothing but setting a world record. I still had something else on my mind. And his initials were J.A.

In mid-November, Justin had a new hobby: jabbing me in the back with a pencil every time I spoke in class. Sometimes it was the eraser end and sometimes it wasn't. I never knew what was coming.

In early December I asked Ms. Wilson to please move me away from Justin, but I could tell she thought that would be a defeat on her part. It would tell the world that she couldn't control Justin Ambrose. So she kept me in the same seat while she tried and tried to bring Justin under control. Meanwhile, my back was starting to look like a waffle.

But at the same time, my karate was getting better and better. I found myself wondering when I would get a chance to let Justin know that I was prepared to defend myself. I was almost looking forward to the next confrontation—wasn't I?

Chapter 5

*B*elieve it or not, now that I was almost ready to fight, Justin started leaving me alone. Except for an occasional pencil poke in the back, nothing happened for the rest of December.

And then Christmas vacation arrived.

From the very first day I knew it was going to be a vacation I'd love. When I woke up and looked out the window on the first morning, the world was buried in six inches of fresh white snow. Then when I stepped on my dad's scale, there was more good news. I measured practically a whole inch taller than I had at the beginning of November.

There was only one problem with a school vacation. Even though *I* was on vacation, my parents weren't. It was a little lonely being home by myself every day. I had to make breakfast myself, and since Carlo is a late sleeper, there usually wasn't much to do until after lunch. But on most days, by the time I was into my second stack of microwave pancakes I had thought of something great to do in the morning.

One day I built a snow fort and later that afternoon Carlo and I totally destroyed it with karate kicks. I spent another whole morning watching old movies on TV—with my head hanging upside down off the edge of the couch. This might not sound like something a really brainy person would do, but believe me, it was just the kind of mental numb-out I needed after four solid months of cramming algebra and American history into my head.

Then Christmas came, and it was great. I got a computer from my parents, along with some software that helps you write your own video game programs. And I got skis. I've never skied before, but I've been wanting to learn for about a year. My parents promised we'd go skiing some weekend in January, and maybe even take a day off from school!

A lot of people gave me books for Christmas, including Carlo. He gave me a copy of the *Guinness Book of World Records* with one of the pages torn out and a note that said, "To be filled in by Carlo Rizzardi in the near future."

Carlo got a present he wasn't expecting, too—not in a million years. His parents gave him a contract they had signed, pledging a matching grant for his World Record Club Sandwich Fund. That meant that however much money he raised on his own for the sliced turkey, his parents would match that amount for the Swiss cheese.

After Christmas, my house settled back to normal—quiet. Just me and my computer. It was so quiet and normal, in fact, that I jumped in my chair when the telephone rang two days after Christmas.

The voice on the other end was gruff and unfriendly. I could tell the person was calling from outside because I could hear cars in the background. "May I speak to Mr. Anderson or Mrs. Anderson?" he said.

Of course I said what kids who are alone in the house are always supposed to say when someone calls. I said, "I'm sorry. My mom and dad can't come to the phone right now."

"Okay," grumbled the voice.

He hung up in a hurry before I could even say, "Could I take a message?"

I went back to my computer, stopping on the way to raid the refrigerator. But I kept thinking about that guy on the phone. Why'd he hang up so fast?

Just then, the front doorbell rang and rang and rang.

"Who is it?" I called through the door. It was too early to be Carlo. "Who's out there?"

There was no answer. I opened the front door with the security chain still hooked. There was no one at the door. I unhooked the door chain and poked my head out. There was no one on the porch.

"Hello?" I called.

That's when the back doorbell started to ring and ring and ring.

I hurried back to the kitchen, but when I got there no one was at the back door. Then the front bell rang again. What's the joke? I wondered.

Living room—kitchen. For a minute I ran back and forth trying to answer the doorbells that kept ringing. But no matter how fast I ran, no one was there. I was starting to get angry . . . and a little scared.

Then a voice called in an eerie half shout, half whisper. "Elliot." The sound seemed to hang in the air outside my house. Hearing my name gave me the chills. How did he know my name? Seconds later he called again from somewhere around the side of the house. "Elliot!"

I ran from window to window, trying to see who was there, but he was always somewhere else.

"Elliot," he called. "Elliot, come out, come out, weasel tail."

That's when I recognized the voice. It was Justin Ambrose. I ran to the living room window and saw the one thing that could

49

ruin my wonderful Christmas vacation. He was standing in our snow-filled front yard like a big ugly blot.

"I know you're in there, Elliot. Come out—now!"

My heart pounded as I reached for the doorknob. I stopped for a moment and looked down at my shaky hands. They couldn't exactly be classified as lethal weapons, but Nick Subotnik had taught me a thing or two. Was it time to teach Justin?

I stepped out onto the porch and decided to try a bluff first to scare him off. "Hi, Justin. Come on in. My parents want to meet you."

"Your parents aren't home," he snapped back with a laugh.

How did he know? "Sure they are," I lied.

" 'I'm sorry, they can't come to the phone right now,' " Justin said, imitating my voice. Then he laughed. "Every kid in the world knows that means nobody's home."

Okay, the bluff didn't work. Like it or not, I was going to have to try something stronger to wipe that sarcastic smile off his face. "Justin, it's vacation," I said, taking a step toward him. "I don't have to see you for another week."

"I missed you, Elliot," he said. "I was sitting at home watching some stupid television show and I said, if I could be doing something else, what would it be? And I didn't have to think twice." He walked closer as he spoke. "I'd like to be hurting Elliot Barf-Bag Anderson."

"Justin, you know what your problem is?" I asked.

But he interrupted me. "Yeah. You."

My feet didn't seem to want to participate. They wouldn't move me even an inch toward Justin. So I stood there and waited. I flexed my hands nervously. They were sweating even in the cold. I tried to remember everything that Nick had taught me.

As Justin approached me, I bowed to him politely, filling my lungs deeply, slowly. Then I stepped off the porch and started moving, circling him. I fixed my hands at chest level, ready to strike.

"Justin," I said, trying to sound more angry than scared, "I'm really sick of you."

He was surprised. He was puzzled. I could see it on his face. He looked at my karate stance and didn't know what to think. He gave me an instant to strike first.

I lashed out at him. My flying fists and elbows and feet attacked as I screamed out a furious cry, "Haieeeeya!"

Every one of my karate chops connected. Pow! Pow! Pow! But Justin didn't even seem to feel them. He didn't flinch—and he certainly didn't fall.

Suddenly I realized I had made a major mistake. And I could tell by the smile that spread across Justin's face that I was about to learn an important lesson in physics. The lesson was: Even if you spend a lot of money on karate lessons, when something that weighs fifty-five pounds hits something that weighs ninety-five pounds, it will never hurt as much as when the process is reversed.

"Swallow this," Justin said, making a fist the size of a brick wall and delivering it right to my face.

A few seconds later, I found myself lying in the cold snow and not remembering exactly how I got there. I sat up and looked around. Justin was gone. As I wiped the snow off my face, I was surprised to see that some of it was red. My nose was bleeding!

I'm going to be dead before I'm twelve, I thought as I lay back in the snow.

Chapter 6

"*I*t wasn't cool, Elliot," Carlo scolded me.

Eight A.M. Great first day back at school so far. I tried to slam my locker door, but my parka sleeve was still hanging out, so it only closed with a thud. "I thought it was the right thing to do under the circumstances," I told Carlo.

He threw up his hands in frustration. "Elliot, you asked Nick Subotnik for your money back."

"So? Karate didn't work."

"You know what you did? You hurt his

feelings," Carlo said, shaking his head at me.

I stuffed the parka sleeve back into my locker and tried to slam the door. No good. Now one of my boots was sticking out. "You want to know what hurt feelings feel like, Carlo? Ask Justin Ambrose to hit you in the face. That's hurt feelings. He knocked the wind out of me and then he made me bleed."

"Elliot, you've got to think positively. If you want something to happen, you have to say, 'I will.' If you say 'I will' enough times, it will happen."

"There's one problem. What if *I'm* thinking positive—I *will* stay out of Justin's way. But *Justin* is thinking positive, too—I *will* beat Elliot's brains out."

Carlo's answer was, "I believe in you, even if you don't." He said it more seriously than he's ever said anything to me, so of course I couldn't argue with him after that.

"Okay, I *will* stay out of Justin's way. And I *will* tell Ms. Wilson to move me away from him immediately."

Carlo and I walked into the classroom

together and gave each other high fives before going to our seats. When I sat down, Justin Ambrose didn't even look up. He was too busy tearing pages out of his math book to notice that I had come in.

That was fine with me, because I wouldn't be sitting there much longer. I couldn't wait for Ms. Wilson to get there. Where was she anyway? The bell had already rung and there was no sign of her anywhere.

For about five more minutes we all sat there talking to each other about Christmas vacation. Then a tall, meaty man in tan corduroy pants and a blue dress shirt with no tie looked into the classroom. At first I thought he was a parent looking for his kid's room or something. I was really surprised when he walked in and started talking to us.

"Quiet down," he said. "My name is Mr. Oakes. Ms. Wilson won't be back for a while. I'm going to be your teacher."

I couldn't believe my ears, and I wasn't the only one. The whole room was totally silent. Finally, Jerrilyn Morris spoke up. "Is Ms. Wilson all right?" she wanted to know. Jerrilyn always asks lots of questions. There could never be too many details in the world for her. Everyone knows she's going to be a great lawyer someday. "What happened to her?" Jerrilyn asked.

"Next time, please raise your hand if you want to speak," Mr. Oakes said. He sounded sharp, but not angry. "Ms. Wilson went to a ski lodge for her winter vacation to learn to ski. The first day she was there, she fell in the parking lot and broke both of her legs."

Shock waves went through the class. It was a lot to take in on the first day after vacation. We started to buzz, but Mr. Oakes held up his hand. "Quiet down," he said. "I want to put my cards on the table right up front. You're still students and this is still a classroom and school will go on." He walked over to Ms. Wilson's desk and started arranging his notebooks and books. "And there's one thing I don't want to hear. I don't want to hear anyone say, 'But we used to do it differently with Ms. Wilson.' I'm sure you did. But I'm your teacher now. You've got to learn how I want things done."

"Will she be back?" asked Jerrilyn.

"I didn't see your hand," Mr. Oakes said, more sharply than before. He walked over to Jerrilyn and stared down at her. "Do you have trouble raising your hand? Do you have a problem with me asking you to raise your hand?"

It was pretty clear to me that he wasn't expecting Jerrilyn to answer his questions. But he certainly wanted her to hear them. He wanted all of us to hear them.

I watched Jerrilyn's face turn red and saw her bite her top lip and stare down at her desk. If there was anyone in this world who knew how I felt when Justin Ambrose was picking on me, it was Jerrilyn Morris.

I felt a sharp jab in my back that made me twitch. I didn't turn around, though. I didn't want to see Justin. But that didn't discourage him from whispering, "Cool dude." He meant Mr. Oakes.

Naturally. Leave it to Justin to get his kicks out of watching a grown-up bullying a kid. Just the fact that Justin liked this new teacher made me want to hate Mr. Oakes. But I couldn't. I always give people a fair chance when I meet them, no matter what

I've heard about them in advance. Carlo says it's one of my worst qualities.

Anyway, Mr. Oakes called the roll since he didn't know any of our names. Then he wrote page numbers for math review on the chalkboard. The room became quiet and the teacher started studying the seating chart while the class worked. I hadn't gone to my algebra class yet, so I didn't have any work.

"The assignment I gave was to do your math, not to stare off into space," I heard Mr. Oakes say. Suddenly I realized he was saying it to me.

"Uh, I use a different math book," I said. I wanted to explain, but I didn't want to brag.

"You're not using the fifth–grade math book," Mr. Oakes half-said and half-asked.

The next voice in the class was Carlo's. "Elliot uses a high–school book," he said proudly.

I'm positive that I saw a look of anger on Mr. Oakes' face for an instant. Our eyes locked.

"That's no excuse for not keeping busy,"

Mr. Oakes said. He pushed back and leaned on the back legs of his desk chair. "This is for everyone's ears: I expect a thousand percent in my class or you're in one-hundred-percent trouble with me. Got that?"

Yeah, I got it—although mathematically speaking it didn't make any sense.

For the rest of the day I tried to stay out of Mr. Oakes' way. Then I thought, "This is weird. I mean, I shouldn't have to worry about my *teacher* picking on me, should I?" I felt like the number of bullies in my life had doubled overnight.

Anyway, when I finally got home from school, I was really looking forward to seeing my mom and dad. You can imagine how bummed out I was when I found this message on the telephone answering machine.

"Hi, Ellie," said my mother's voice. "Sorry I missed you. Guess I called too soon. Dad and I won't be home until late tonight. I've asked Ben Blake to come at 5:00 to baby-sit. I'll be in the office in about an hour, so I'll call you then. I love you. Bye."

"Bye," I said to the answering machine.

Ben Blake was a ninth grader who lived up the street and had been my baby sitter for a few years. I don't need a sitter in the daytime, of course. But at night my dad, the psychologist, still thinks a fifth grader should have some "moral support."

Around dinner time, the doorbell rang. At first I wondered if it was Justin again, but I looked out the window and, to my relief, saw Ben.

"Hi, Ben," I said, opening the door.

"Hi, Elliot," said Ben, kicking the snow off his track shoes.

"Want some dinner?" I asked.

"I already ate," said Ben. "What are you having?"

Keeping a conversation going with Ben was a lot like hitting a balloon around. It sailed when you first hit it, but then it immediately started dropping. Ben was a certified jock, a star at every sport he tried. He was tall and strong and fast. But he wasn't great when it came to studying.

I put two frozen dinners in the microwave. Ben sat down at the table and started doing his homework.

"Oh, nuts," he said, reading a book and leaning his cheek on his fist. "Oh, nuts, nuts."

"What are you reading, Ben? The story of peanut butter?"

Ben laughed. I forgot to mention he has a good sense of humor.

"Algebra. Just wait till you have it."

I lifted the cover of his book. "I'm using this book now," I said.

"You're smart, Elliot," said Ben with a whistle. "I admire you."

I tried not to look surprised, but I knew I failed. A ninth grader, a high school sports superstar, was saying *he* admired *me*?

"Algebra's not that hard," I said. "It's very logical." I sat down next to Ben and explained the first problem to him. After that, he did the next three problems on his own. But he didn't look happy about it.

When the food came out of the microwave, Ben put down his pencil. "Elliot," he said, "I've got a great idea. I'll pay you a dollar a day if you'll teach me algebra. And two dollars more a week if you won't tell anyone that I'm being tutored by a fifth grader."

"Wow!" I said. "Deal!"

We shook hands and I ran to call Carlo to tell him the news—that I'd have some money to contribute to the world's tallest club sandwich. It was a weird conversation, though, since I couldn't tell Carlo exactly how I was going to earn the money. But he didn't really care.

After dinner, I decided to trust Ben with a secret of my own.

"Ben, what would you do if someone picked on you?" I asked.

Ben thought for a long while, and finally said, "I don't know. No one's ever picked on me."

Of course not. He was tall. He'd probably always been tall.

"I know what the coach told me to do when someone tried to intimidate me on the football field."

"Great. Professional advice. Tell me," I said anxiously.

"Hit 'em someplace that hurts."

I smiled a weak smile. I had already tried that strategy on Justin and had filed it under ESTD—Easier Said Than Done!

Chapter 7

*T*he best thing I can say about February is that it was the shortest month of the year. I don't want to say more about it because then I'll start remembering all the things that happened to me, most of them at the hands of Justin Ambrose.

At least March promised to be better.

Early in the month Mr. Oakes assigned a new class project that got everyone excited.

"This month," Mr. Oakes announced, "we're going to be studying our own city, Greatdale."

By March everyone in class had gotten

used to the way Mr. Oakes talked to us. He never seemed really happy about anything that he said to us or we said to him. But he did tell people when they were doing their work well and he told them when they weren't. It was easy to tell which he preferred. "Mary Alice," he'd say, "good report. Well written." Or he'd say, "Elliot, push yourself harder next time. You won't be happy if you don't."

Anyway, the new project sounded great to me, even if Mr. Oakes didn't sound excited when he told us. One of the best things was that it was a video project.

"I'm dividing the class into four study groups," Mr. Oakes explained. "Each group will be allowed to use the school's video camcorder for three days. I don't care what you photograph as long as, when you play your tape for the class, it tells us something we didn't know about Greatdale."

But the absolute best part of this project was that you-know-who wasn't in my group.

From then on, a special meeting of each group became part of the daily schedule. The group I was in included Carlo and four other kids. At our first meeting we tried to decide what we wanted to shoot.

"Whatever it is, I want to be the guy talking into the microphone," Carlo announced, giving us one of his star-quality smiles.

"Now that's a big surprise," said Lionel Wilson. Lionel had major braces on his top and bottom teeth, plus a retainer, which meant that people standing too close to him usually got a spit shower when he spoke.

"Hey, Elliot," said Luis Fernandez, nudging me with his elbow, "are you sure you don't want to be in Justin's group?"

"Yeah," teased Barbara O'Malley. "I thought you guys went everywhere together."

Hank Tetone tried to stop laughing long enough to say something. I wished he hadn't bothered. "They stick together because Justin always has his fist *stuck* in Elliot's face."

I tried to laugh, to make everyone think I was a good sport about their jokes. After all, I had made it through ten years of short jokes. But Elliot-bashing was catching on in my class. I knew these guys were mostly teasing, though. If they knew they were really hurting my feelings, they'd probably stop—eventually. Meanwhile, I sat back in my chair, feeling smaller every minute.

"Come on, you guys," Carlo said, trying to change the subject. "Are we going to get some planning done here or what?"

"That would be a first," said Lionel.

Suddenly, Barbara O'Malley's eyes opened wide with excitement behind her glasses. "That's a *great* idea, Lionel!" she said. Barbara thought everything Lionel said was a great idea. "We could call our tape 'Firsts'! We could go around and do the famous firsts in Greatdale. Like the first building in Greatdale."

Actually, it *was* a great idea. Everyone started naming firsts we could put on the tape.

"The first school in town," said Luis.

"The first book in the library," I said.

"How about first base on the playground?" said Hank with his big, snorting laugh.

By the end of the meeting, we had some great ideas. We made a final list, and at the top of it was the first person to die in Great-dale. We'd have to go to the old cemetery to shoot his or her gravestone, and we were going to find out everything we could about that person. We also planned to shoot the first house in Greatdale. If we couldn't show the house because it had been torn down or something, we'd show where it used to be. And we were going to try to get Stand-ford Whitaker, the richest man in town, on videotape because everyone always said that he still had the *first* dollar he ever earned. Once we had our list of "firsts" put together we were ready to try our hands at video-taping.

A few days later we got our chance. After giving us a quick lesson in operating the camera, Mr. Oakes sent the six of us outside to practice shooting on videotape.

Hank Tetone was the biggest kid, so we made him the cameraman. At first nobody really knew what to do or say in front of the camera. We kind of looked at each other a lot, laughed, and pushed each other around.

"You guys are so immature," Carlo said, shaking his head.

"Do *you* know what to do, Carlo?" asked Barbara O'Malley.

"First of all, forget about the camera," Carlo said. "Pretend it's not a camera. Pretend it's someone you know."

"You can pretend it's Lionel, Barbara," teased Luis.

Barbara and Lionel both blushed at that remark and Hank quickly snapped on the camcorder to record their total embarrassment.

"Watch me," Carlo said. He looked straight into the camera and smiled a friendly smile. "Hi, how're ya doing? Well, this is my school. I know it looks like a typical American school, but it isn't. Weird things go on here."

We all followed Carlo as he walked around the playground. He was doing exactly what he said—talking to the camera as if it were a friend. He was great at it.

"Look at that," Carlo said. "See that cat sitting over there?"

Hank aimed the camera at a big calico cat that was sunning itself on the empty slide.

"You know what it means when a cat comes to visit our playground, don't you?"

said Carlo. "It means we'll be having spaghetti with *meat* sauce in the cafeteria tomorrow."

"Totally gross," Barbara O'Malley moaned. "You're sick, Carlo."

"Okay, okay," Hank said, handing the camcorder to me. "My turn."

Hank stood in front of me and I pointed the camera up at him. "Hi," he began. "Well, uh, our group is making a videotape about famous firsts here in Greatdale. Well, a famous first happened right here. This is where Justin Ambrose beat Elliot Anderson to a bloody pulp for the *first* time."

I couldn't believe my ears. What was he doing? "Hey!" I said, but I was drowned out by everyone laughing.

"That's not funny," Carlo said. But everyone just ignored him.

"And over here—over here," cried Lionel Wilson, laughing and spitting as he talked, "that's where Elliot *first* begged and pleaded with Justin for mercy. But did he get it?"

"Noooo!" the four of them said in unison.

Suddenly it was a contest. They were trying to see who could laugh the loudest and make up the worst story about me. I turned off the camera and glared at them.

"Come on, stop it, you guys," Carlo said.

"I know, I know," said Luis Fernandez, "let's go to the boys' locker room and show where Justin *first* pushed Elliot's face into a pile of dirty towels!"

It was the worst day of my life. A month ago, these guys used to feel a little sympathy for what Justin was putting me through. Now they had practically crawled down to his level.

My hands were sweaty and my legs were shaking. I wanted to run into the nearest hole in the ground. I glared at the four of them, who were suddenly looking very surprised.

Then the camera seemed to fly out of my hands. I looked up and Mr. Oakes was standing behind me, holding the camera and giving the six of us an angry stare.

"What's going on?" he asked. "Whatever it is, it's too loud to be productive. Get inside, all of you."

"But the tape," Luis said, giving me a quick, embarrassed look.

"You're through taping for today," Mr. Oakes said. He marched back to the school building, carrying the camcorder with the videotape still inside.

Chapter 8

I went straight home after school that day. I didn't even want to be with Carlo. It was bad enough that Justin had terrorized me for the past seven months. But now practically everyone in school was joining in. I basically wanted to disappear off the face of the earth.

When I got home, there was a message on the answering machine.

I hit the play button, hoping it wouldn't be my mom or dad saying they weren't coming home.

BEEP! Then a voice spoke. "This is a message for Elliot," it said.

It wasn't my parents and that made me happy. But I couldn't believe who it was.

"This is your teacher, Mr. Oakes. Come to school early tomorrow morning for a conference. I want to talk to you about the videotape I found in the camcorder. See you at the gym at 7:30 sharp."

I couldn't imagine what he was going to say to me, but I had a feeling I didn't want to hear it.

When I got to the gym at 7:15 the next morning, Mr. Oakes was already there. He was dressed in sweats, and shooting baskets. When he saw me he stopped, walked over to the bleachers, and drank from a small bottle of water.

"Elliot," he said. "I always work out before school. Come on. Let's shoot some hoops."

We took turns. He tried jump shots, hook shots, and lay-ups. In between each of his shots, he'd bounce the ball to me and I'd throw the ball as hard as I could. Sometimes it hit the backboard, but most of the time it just sort of arced through the air and came down again without hitting anything. My "airball" percentage is pretty high.

"I looked at the videotape your group shot yesterday," he said.

I already knew that. Why was he taking so long to get to the point?

"And I called Ms. Wilson last night to get the details about what had gone on between you and Justin Ambrose while she was still here." He made his shot and the ball zipped through the net. "Doesn't sound like it's been a fun year."

For the first time I felt that he wasn't criticizing me or even judging me. That made it easier for me to talk to him, although "Yeah" was the only thing I said just then. I threw a ball that bounced around on the rim and slipped through the net.

I looked over and Mr. Oakes was smiling. He finished his bottle of water in a couple of big, quick gulps. "You know, I could make your problems with Justin disappear faster than you can blink," he said with a self-satisfied grin.

I practically moaned with relief. "That would be great," I said.

But the grin quickly disappeared, and he

looked at me as if I had misunderstood him. "But I'm not going to do it, Elliot. It's your problem and you have to solve it."

I walked over to him with the basketball under my arm. "Don't you think I'd like to? I've tried. I can't. I'm not big enough, okay?" I put the ball down and let it roll to him.

"I'm going to tell you a story about when I was in the fifth grade. Sit down, Elliot. It's a long story."

I sat down on the bleachers while Mr. Oakes told his story. As he spoke, he kept trying to spin the ball on his index finger.

"It was a regular kind of fifth grade class. The girls were well-behaved and the boys were boys. I think we had one smart kid in our class, but he wouldn't have been any competition for you, Elliot. There was another kid—I'm not going to use his name, because every class has one and his name is not important. But he was a bully, Elliot, pure and simple, a bully from the time he was in kindergarten. He had always been the biggest kid in the class, the kind with lots of meat on him and lots of anger inside. This kid never liked the world or anything living in it. He went after everyone in class, one by one. Boy, girl, it didn't matter. He just liked to pick fights. 'You think you're tough—well I think you're a pile of six-day-old slime.' That's what he used to say."

"Sounds a lot like someone I know," I said.

"Don't interrupt," said Mr. Oakes. "The thing is, every year this bully started a fight with everyone in the class. He acted like the toughest thing since school-cafeteria meat loaf. He pounded everything that walked in that classroom, except—" Then he paused.

"Except what?" I instantly asked.

"Well, except there was this new kid who moved into the school district and found himself in the same class with the bully. No one could believe it, but the new kid never got a minute of grief from the bully."

"That's nice, Mr. Oakes. He must have been big," I said. "It's a whole different story when you're small."

"I know that, Elliot. I know that for a fact. You see, this new kid, he was real small."

"Smaller than I am?" I asked.

"Elliot, I've eaten steaks bigger than this

kid was," said Mr. Oakes, actually laughing. "The kid was a real shrimp, but the bully never touched him. I mean, when the shrimp walked into the classroom, the bully shut up and watched him carefully. The bully never walked in front of the shrimp if he could help it."

"Why?"

"That's what everyone in class wanted to know. It drove them crazy. Did the shrimp know a secret about the bully? What kind of mysterious power did he have? What kind of threat did he use against this kid who had terrorized the other kids for years?

"One day, the class cornered the shrimp on the playground to find out. It was a strange sight: ten, fifteen big kids all standing around a skinny little short kid, everyone squeezing close so they all could hear what he was going to say. 'Why doesn't he push you and pick on you and take your lunch money and ruin your life?' they asked.

"The shrimp didn't have to think twice about it. 'Because,' he said, 'I don't let him.' "

Mr. Oakes turned and tossed the basketball in a hook shot. He sank a three-pointer. We watched the basketball bounce across the gym floor. The story was over and we were both quiet.

"Okay, I get it," I said. "You think I should stand up to Justin—I'll get pounded for sure but at least I'll be standing up."

"No, you don't get it, Elliot. Bullies only do what people allow them to do. What I learned in the fifth grade is that the kid who stands up doesn't get pounded," said Mr. Oakes.

That sounded like a contradiction to me. It was my experience that if you stand up and ask someone to pound you, you get exactly what you ordered.

I was about to say that when Mr. Oakes said, "You'd better head for class. I'm going to take a quick shower."

We started to leave the gym through opposite doors, but I turned around with one question I had to ask.

"I know about stories like this, Mr. Oakes," I called back to him. "You were the shrimp, weren't you?"

He smiled at me and I thought I was going to have to settle for that as my answer.

"No, Elliot," Mr. Oakes said, "I wasn't the shrimp. I was the bully."

I didn't know what to say. At first I thought, I should have guessed it from the way he acted in class sometimes. But after talking to him like this, I also saw the other side of Mr. Oakes, the side that tried his best not to be a tough guy but maybe sometimes just couldn't help it.

And he did tell me the story, didn't he? He wanted to help *me* deal with Justin. And that's exactly what I was going to have to do—eventually. But not today. Maybe I'd be five inches taller tomorrow.

◆ Chapter 9 ◆

"**A**re you sure you want to do this, Elliot?" Carlo asked.

"No, I don't *want* to do this. But I've *got* to do it."

It was a beautiful April day. Flowers were budding and blooming everywhere you looked. Birds sang in the sunshine of the warm, late afternoon. In short, it was the perfect day for revenge.

It was a Friday, two weeks after my talk with Mr. Oakes. I had thought a lot about the bully and the shrimp. It was obvious that I couldn't sit around anymore waiting and hoping for a flock of vultures to find their way to Justin's house and take care of my problem for me. I had to deal with him myself.

In a strange way, Carlo was the one who encouraged me the most. Recently, Carlo had been changing. He stopped talking so much about setting the tallest club sandwich world record. He stopped talking about it because he didn't have time to boast or brag. He was getting serious. This wasn't just a comedy bit with him now. He was really going to make it happen.

In addition to the matching fund, Carlo got his parents to agree to pay him four dollars for every A he got on his report card. I'm sure they thought it was a safe bet on their part, because Carlo's grades were usually toward the middle of the alphabet rather than the beginning. But Carlo fooled everyone and transformed into a study-aholic. He and I got together after school every Monday, Wednesday, and Friday and spent the whole time studying! When he wasn't studying, he was making more money by doing chores for neighbors, recycling newspapers and plastic bottles, or doing anything else someone would pay him for.

Something else changed, too: Carlo's attitude about me. Before, he was embarrassed about my frequent collisions with Justin's fists. He kept urging me to take karate or do something else to get back at Justin. But Carlo stopped saying those things and I think he stopped being embarrassed that I was getting pounded. He was going to be my friend, no matter what I could or couldn't do.

That's what gave me the courage to try, because I knew that no matter what happened, Carlo and I would always be best friends.

That's also why he volunteered to help me with my plan.

"That's Justin's house," I said, pointing to a small, red brick house across the street from where Carlo and I were hiding behind a large oak tree. "I know he's home alone."

"How do you know?" Carlo asked.

"Because before you got here, I called and asked to speak to his parents and he said they couldn't come to the phone."

"Which means they're not there," said Carlo.

I nodded my head. "I'll ring the front

bell and you ring the back bell, or knock on the door if there isn't a bell. Then hide when he comes out."

We set the plan into motion with a high five for good luck. Then we zipped across the street, straight for Justin's house.

I took a deep breath. I knew once I pushed the button, there was no going back. I did it. I rang the front bell four times and jumped off the porch, into some bushes. I heard the front door open. With the door open, I could hear the back bell start to ring. The front door closed, and I leaped back onto the porch and started ringing the bell again.

I had just made it back into the bushes when the door opened again, sooner than the last time. Justin must have been running between the doors, just like I had. When I heard the back bell ring and the front door close again, I ran around the house throwing small pebbles on all the windows. I caught up with Carlo in back and we both ran to the front yard.

"I'll bet he's really mad, Elliot," Carlo warned me.

"Let's give him a test and see how mad he is," I said with a smile.

"Sure," Carlo said, taking a few steps back toward the street.

"Justin! Justin! Hey, rhino breath! Hey, fungus head!" I shouted at the top of my lungs.

Justin Ambrose came slowly out of his house, looking around. It was obvious that *I* wasn't what he was expecting to find.

"Elliot?" he said, with a laugh. He stood at the top of his porch steps and relaxed his fists. Nothing to worry about. It was only me. But he was surprised. "What are you doing here?"

"I wanted to tell you something, Justin," I said.

"Go ahead and tell me, Elliot," he said, squeezing his hands into fists. "But stand closer. . . . at arm's length."

I walked across his yard to be closer to his porch and to him, knowing that I was walking into an ambush. "Okay. Hit me. Knock me down."

"Are you kidding? Are you nuts or something?"

"Yeah, I'm nuts. So go ahead. Hit me. You know what I'll do?"

"Bleed," answered Justin.

"Wrong, and that's what I wanted to tell you, Justin." I was so nervous, the words were tumbling out of my mouth as fast as I could say them. "I'll get back up, and if you hit me again, I'll get up again, and I'll do it again and again. And one of these times, I'm going to hit you so hard and plant you in the ground so deep you're going to think you're a tulip bulb!"

"Go away, Elliot," Justin said. "I'll have to beat you up tomorrow."

I almost didn't want to believe my ears— but I could hear the threat draining out of his voice. And not only that, he stuffed his fists into his jeans pockets. He was squirming.

"Well," I said, "are you going to fight me or not, Justin?"

"Leave me alone, Elliot," Justin said, backing away toward his front door.

"What for? *You* never listened when I said that to you," I said. "Why have you been picking on me the *whole* year?"

Justin sneered at me. "I would have picked on you last year, too, but I didn't know you well enough," he joked.

"How about giving me a straight answer for once?" I snapped. "What did I do to you? One stupid baseball catch?"

"You want a straight answer?" he said. He leaped off the porch and charged toward me, then stopped six feet away. "I *hate* you. Everything's great for you. You've got lots of friends. The teachers all love you and you get good grades. Hey—that's not how things work, you know? That's not the real world. So I had to show you."

We weren't shouting at each other then. Maybe we were looking at each other for the first time.

"Yeah, right. Everything's perfect for me, except I'm still not big enough to ride most of the roller coasters in the United States. I have to buy clothes that are too small if I want to look like I've grown. I'd love to smack a fly ball over the fence, but I'm lucky if I get it past the infield. And I never see my parents before dinnertime."

"Why not?" Justin asked, scowling.

"They work. They're busy all the time."

"My mom works all the time, too," Justin said. "And my dad moved out last fall."

"It's a bummer, isn't it?" I said. We didn't say anything for a minute. Then I asked with a half smile, "So you don't want to fight me?"

Justin shook his head. "I'll give you a break this time," he said weakly.

Carlo and I practically flew all the way home.

"You know, if you were taller, Elliot, you'd have the makings of a great bully," Carlo said with a laugh. "Or a lion tamer."

"Lion tamers never turn their backs on the lions," I said cautiously. Maybe I had won the battle, but that didn't mean the war was over.

But all weekend I was in a fantastic mood. I didn't even get on my dad's scale once. Why spoil a great weekend with bad news?

First thing Monday morning our gym class had its first baseball game of the spring season. I was anxious to see if I could hit the ball out of the field yet. But I was also anxious to see how Justin was going to act.

Would things really be different now? Justin kept to himself and didn't look at me, so it was hard to tell.

The game was moving along toward a happy ending. My team was winning by one run going into the bottom of the last inning. Two out. The other team had its fastest runner on second base—Barbara O'Malley. Then Justin Ambrose came to the plate.

Wait a minute, I said to myself. What's happening? Have I stepped back in time? I was standing in right field again—just like at the beginning of the year—when Justin smacked the first pitch and it sailed right toward me.

I watched it fly in slow motion, thinking, this isn't happening. Should I catch the ball and put him out—and risk another beating from Justin? Or should I let my team lose? Hey, it was only a game in P.E.

The ball began to drop. I calculated its speed and then my instincts clicked in. I took off running. When I couldn't run anymore, I flew. I leaped into the air and came down with a thump—with the ball in my glove.

We won the game and a few friends carried me back to the school building on their shoulders.

But Justin was waiting for me when I got to my desk.

"See you after school," he said, pointing a finger at me.

My heart sank a little, but I pushed it back up, saying to myself, "I won't let him, that's all."

After school, Carlo and I started for home and found Justin standing in our way at the bike racks.

I took a deep breath and marched up to stand toe to toe with him. "Don't try anything," I said.

Justin stared at me and then looked away. "Good catch, Elliot. You beat us fair and square. Maybe I should be on your team next time."

"Sounds okay to me," I said cautiously.

Justin looked at Carlo next. "I heard you guys are trying to get into the *Guinness Book of World Records*."

"We're *this* close," Carlo said, holding his index finger about an inch from his thumb.

"Uh-huh," said Justin, reaching into his pocket.

Carlo and I both flinched. What was he pulling out? A rock? A missile? No, it was a ten-dollar bill.

"If I put up some money, think I could help?"

Carlo's eyes began to sparkle. "An investor? What do you say, Elliot?" Carlo asked, taking the money from Justin's hand.

I didn't know what to say. I'd just spent a whole year trying to get away from this guy. Was he trying to trick us? Or was it crazy to think he really wanted to be my friend?

When I didn't answer right away, Justin snapped, "Forget it," and grabbed at his money.

But Carlo jerked it away and waved the ten-dollar bill at me. "Relax, Justin. Come on, Elliot—what do you say? It's ten bucks."

"Well, we could use the money," I said slowly.

"Absolutely," Carlo said, nodding. "And we'll need some help building the sandwich, too."

"We will?" I asked, surprised.

"Sure," Carlo said, folding the ten-dollar bill and putting it into his pocket. "Hey, I'm going to be climbing up a twenty-foot ladder to build this thing. Someone's got to hold the ladder steady, right? And what about those mayonnaise jars? You know how hard they are to open. Wouldn't you like some help, Elliot?"

I could see in Carlo's eyes that I didn't have a chance. If Dracula had ten dollars, Carlo wouldn't think twice about letting him work on the sandwich.

"So am I in on the sandwich?" Justin asked.

"Sure," I said with a small sigh.

"Great!" Justin said, and actually smiled at me.

Thanks to Carlo and Mr. Oakes—and a whole weird sequence of events that I'd never have believed if you'd told me at the beginning of the year—it looked like Justin and I were going to be buddies after all.

Maybe there *were* some advantages to being the smallest kid in the fifth grade!